S. DeWitt Hubbell

Satin Slippers

And other Poems

S. DeWitt Hubbell

Satin Slippers
And other Poems

ISBN/EAN: 9783744765923

Printed in Europe, USA, Canada, Australia, Japan

Cover: Foto ©Andreas Hilbeck / pixelio.de

More available books at **www.hansebooks.com**

SATIN SLIPPERS,

AND

OTHER POEMS.

BY

S. DE WITT HUBBELL,

(D'ORVILLE.)

RED BLUFF:

PRINTED BY CHALMERS & BISHOP,

MDCCCLXI.

TO THE

HON. J. GRANVILLE DOLL,

EVER THE WARM-HEARTED FRIEND OF EVERY ENTERPRISE THAT TENDS TO ADVANCE

THE WELFARE OF HIS FELLOW MEN; AND TO

The Citizens of Tehama County,

AMONG WHOM HE HAS LIVED SO MANY HAPPY YEARS, AND TO WHOSE KIND

APPRECIATION HE COMMITS IT,

THIS LITTLE VOLUME

IS GRATEFULLY DEDICATED BY

THE AUTHOR.

SATIN SLIPPERS.

A cobbler sat in a dim-lit stall,
Stitching away with needle and awl;
Making a pair of slippers small.
Two little slippers of satin white,
With soles of cork so thin and light,
And a lining of silk all smooth and bright.
From morning to eve at his task he plies,
Till finished these slippers of marvellous size,
So dainty and neat with their ribbon ties.
As the lamps were lit, the cobbler hied
To the gorgeous mansion where did reside,
Miss Florence Ellen Alice McBride.

O! she was as fair as the lily white,
When the dew-drop lies on its cheek at night;
But proud and haughty as the devil, quite.
Her eyes were blue, and her teeth were pearls,
Her head was covered with auburn curls,
And her lips were like leaves the moss rose unfurls.
Her arms were round, and her fingers slim,
Her ankles were small, and neat and trim,
With the smallest of feet attached to them.
O! such an exquisite, dear little foot
That none of her friends could wear her boot,
Though they tugged till their faces were black as soot;
And, as she danced, you could scarcely tell
When it touched the floor, 'twas handled so well.

Old McBride was as rich as a Jew,
Or, as some did say, he was rich as two,
And all of his kin were as rich as he,
Down to cousins of the tenth degree.
He was puffy, and stout, with little red eyes,
And his breathing resembled a porpoise's sighs.
He was bow-legged and short, with a bullet head,
And a crop of hair of the coarsest red.
He was pompous and grave; looked knowing and wise,
As he twirled his seals of a monstrous size;
His name was extremely heavy on 'Change,
And his credit had an astounishing range.

Madame M. had departed this sphere,
The morn that our heroine did appear,
Which old Mac thought so devilish queer,
That one day, over a pint of beer,
He told to the parson—a pious man,
Who of her funeral drew up the plan—
That he thought it was strange his Polly Ann
Should go off and leave him in such a way,
When he scarcely had needed her till that day;
And now he was left to worry alone
With a squalling babe scarce two days grown.
Then he scratched his head, and swore an oath
That, thank his luck! he'd enough for both,
And, in spite of her mother's loss, that she,
Should be all that his daughter ought to be!

Three nurses sat at her cradle side;
Number one the mother's place supplied,
Number two rocked the cradle when she cried,
And the third was on hand for what might betide.
But now, as all babies are worried through
The same course of life the first year or two;
Have each one their squallings, spankings and pap,
With bumpings on floor, and pinchings on lap,
Miss McBride's baby life it is needless to tell,
Save, that on such treatment she throve wondrous well.

At the ripe age of eight she was sent off to school
In a coach and four, to be taught by strict rule
To dance and to sing, to curtsey and faint,
To bang a piano, and daub with oil paint ;
Through Society's jam to swing with a grace
Her steel-ribbed skirts to the very best place ;
To tease and torment, to flirt and to slander,
To sneer with contempt at all mention of candor ;
In short, to a school where most wonderful pains
Are taken to develop all else but the brains ;
And, as for the heart, the seventieth rule
Says that " no such thing is allowed in the school."
After eight years of life in that "finishing college,"
Miss McBride was declared perfected in knowledge,
And sent back to her pa, as a young lady, whose skill
Could turn a " Jack" for husband from the world's " deck,"
        at will.

Miss Florence Ellen Alice McBride
Was seated her toilet table beside,
While her waiting maid, with a skillful pride,
Arranged each curl of her auburn hair
To gracefully fall on the neck so fair.
O! that toilet table, of rosewood made,
Was a real bijou, for which old Mac paid
A fabulous sum, so I am told,
For its surface was inlaid with pearl and gold.
It held perfumes and extracts, divinely sweet,
With soap for the hands and soap for the feet,
Soap for the face, and soap for the arms,
Cosmetics and washes to add to her charms ;
With brushes and combs of all shapes and sizes,
And powders and pastes beyond ones surmises ;
With hundreds of pins, large, middling and small,
And hundreds of boxes to hold each and all.
Besides numbers of things, whose use none can tell
Save a beautiful, fashionable, young city belle.

Miss Florence had lately returned from her school.
And, as bon-ton life is all done up by rule,

An old maiden aunt, of sixty, about,
Had promised to bring the young lady "out,"
And to give to her entrance into life a tone,
Had consented to act as Miss Flor's chaperone;
And, as this was the night for her splendid *debut*.
She was "making up," the scene to go through.

At last she is dressed, and lovely she seems,
All curls, and all smiles, like the angels of dreams,
Or the sweet little girls we meet in romance,
Whom we know to be myths, but still allow to entrance.
She steps into her carriage with the elderly aunt,
Who looks wretchedly solemn as becomes one so gaunt.
The sweet little slippers, the pets of our song,
In a casket of pearl are carried along.
With the flesh colored hose, so fine and so thin,
Which young ladies delight to encase their limbs in,
And which, when drawn tight on a leg round and small,
Of all woman's lures is the surest of all.
These things, according to etiquette's law,
In the ball dressing room on their feet all must draw,
And arrange the stray curls, disturbed on the way,
Before making their grand and imposing *entrée*.

The ball it was grand, for all of the fashion
Had turned out in force, and were crowding and crashing.
The ladies were all most superbly dressed,
But Miss Florence McBride far *outstripped* all the rest.
There was music above, and dancing below,
And hundreds of feet and tongues on the go.
There was flirting of fans, and handkerchiefs fine,
Till the air, *a la Française*, smelt deadly divine.
There was smashing of hoops, and tearing of dresses,
And a wonderful coming down of silk tresses.
The heat it was charming, so said young and old,
And the fainting away was a sight to behold.
There was treading on corns and squeezing of waists
And a rapid dissolving of rouges and pastes.
In fact, there was comfort, enjoyment and mirth,
That ever was found on this dancing-crazed earth.

At last, as the day was beginning to dawn,
The ball came to an end, lest the clear, honest morn
Should peep in at the window, and see, with surprise,
So many pale faces, and weak, pallid eyes.
Miss Florence McBride, in her carriage snug stowed,
By three of her partners, most terribly blowed,
Rode home to her father's, where going to bed,
She enjoyed the hard throbbings of a hot, aching head.

For two years thus through life she danced,
Flirted and flounced, and hopped and pranced,
Had admirers a score, but lovers none ;
For love is a thing frowned down by the " ton."
At length, one day, came a white, whiskered thing,
With a huge moustache, and a diamond ring.
He was dressed and fashioned up to the rule,
And some relation to Doestick's " Damphool."
He asked Miss Flor, with a simper sweet,
At how much she valued her hand and feet ?
She named the sum, and the bargain was made,
With old Mac's disinterested aid.
The wedding was fine, the trousseau grand,
And the papers blazoned it through the land :
" The groom was handsome—the bride a queen,
'Twas the finest affair that ever was seen."
But not half of its splendors could ever be told,—
This wonderful wedding of whiskers and gold.

As a maid, Miss McBride had danced much before,
As a wife, she danced, at least, as much more,
And her husband, who sickened of so much show,
Would cheerfully give her up to a beau.
Five years of their married life thus pass'd,
One year very much resembling the last :
At the Club, her husband his time spent all,
While Madame, the nights would pass at a ball.
But one day there came a financial smash,
And old Mac went down with the rest in the crash,
And the loss of his wealth so affected his brain,
That the old gentleman never recovered again.

"Damphool's" relation, having spent every red,
With another man's wife, robbed her husband, and fled.

*   *   *   *   *

On a rude bed of straw, a garret within,
Lies a half naked form, starved, wasted, and thin,
With the traces of beauty still lingering where
Down the shrivelled neck rolls the thin, matted hair.
Alone, and dying, with the cold winter wind
Moaning and whistling through the old, broken blind;
No lamp, and no fire, save one feeble light,
That hardly dispels the darkness of night;
With the cold form of Death lying down by her side,
Is all that remains of Miss Florence McBride.
On her thin, little feet some caprice, to-night,
Has half fastened a pair of slippers white;
Soiled, worn, and in tatters, full well do they mate
With her own sad, dark and desolate fate.
Poor, wretched being! she's danced her last "set,"
For Death, as a partner, his victim has met;
And the music above, is the drive of the sleet
On the roof, as he finds that partner a seat;
And the carriage that takes her, at morn, away,
Is the hearse with its plumes and sable array,
To a couch, where no dreams, or throbbing headache
Disturbs the slumber from which none awake.

A SONG OF SPRING.

The golden violet of spring time
   On the red land lifts its head,
And the sunbeam amongst the clover
   Tells that winter has fled.

Though the snow 'mid old " Yoly's" wrinkles
   Looks cold and white through the air ;
And the midnight leaves frozen kisses,
   On old "Lassen's" temples bare ;

Yet, hither the sunlight cometh,
   In smiles so merry and bright,
That frosts, if still lingering near us,
   Steal by with a footstep light.

The earth, like some lady of fashion,
   At toilette passes the hours ;
Her torn robes and gray tresses trimming
   With buds, and leaves, and flowers.

She looks in her deep azure mirror,
   Then smiles and gazes once more,
In the pride of the beauty they've lent her ;
   So old and withered before.

Rejoice ! for the glorious spring time
   Has come, and the bird and the bee,
On feathered and silken pinion,
   Woo flower, and shrub, and tree.

Through yon cloud of silver, whose whiteness
   Is sheening from heaven, afar,
The light of the moon falls, blended
   With the glory of many a star.

A DIRGE.

Moan, moan, moan—
    As you sway in the winds, old oak ;
And a cry goes forth on the midnight air
    From a heart all shattered and broke.

Still darker the midnight grows,
    And the woods in the shade sink deep ;
But the heart that is ever calling the lost
    Knows not of the sweetness of sleep.

Gone ! gone ! gone !—
    'Tis all that my soul doth know ;
And, oh ! the sorrows of those that are left
    To mourn for the ones that go !

The red right arm of the sun,
    With a sceptre of golden light,
Will drive the darkness, at morn, away,
    And scatter the shadows of night.

Yet, there'll never come back to me,
    The light that has gone from my soul ;
But on through the day and on through the night
    A funeral bell will toll.

Toll, toll, toll—
    A muffled, funeral bell,
Ever ringing within my heart,
    For the lost, a dismal knell.

My soul, in its wildness of grief,
    On the name of the lost doth cry ;
And my heart will wait for an answering voice—
    Perchance it may come, ere I die.

EL RODEO.*

Few are the sunny years, Fair Land of Gold,
    That round thy brow their circlet bright have twined ;
Yet, each thy youthful form hath still enrolled
    In wondrous garb of peace and wealth combined.
Few are the years, since old Hispania's sons
    Reared here their Missions, tolled the chapel bell,
Subdued the native with their priestly guns,
    To bear the cross of God, and man, as well.

Oft have the holy fathers careless stood
    Within thy valleys, then a blooming waste ;
Or heedless toiled along the mountain flood,
    That, rich with treasure, downward foamed and raced.
Those times and scenes have all long passed away,
    Before the white man's wisdom-guided tread,
As fly the shades before the steps of Day,
    When in the East he lifts his radiant head.

But still, thy valleys and thy mountains teem
    With customs, common to the race of old ;
Like Indian names bequeathed to lake and stream,
    They'll live while Time his restless reign shall hold.
'Tis of one such that I essay to sing ;
    A custom much in vogue, and, no doubt, dear
To all who brood 'neath Spain's maternal wing,
    Or "swing a lass"—they call it El Rodeo.

Last night, at sunset, down the stream, I saw
    The dark vaqueros† ride along the plain,

---

* The common pronunciation, (Rodere), is given in the poem to this word, though, perhaps, it may not be strictly correct.

† Bucharos—men who herd stock, and perform other duties on a stock ranch. They are generally Mexicans or Chilenos.

B

With jingling spur, and bit, and jaquima,*
  And snake-like lariats†—scarce e'er hurled in vain.
The steeds they rode were champing on the bit,
  The agile riders lightly sat their "trees,"
And many a laugh, and waif of Spanish wit,
  Made merry music on the evening breeze.

Far out beyond the hills their course they took,
  And, where there lies, in early summer days,
A lake, or slough, or, chance, a pebbly brook,
  The cayote saw their camp-fire wildly blaze.
All night they lay beneath its lurid glare,
  Till had upsprung morn's beauteous herald star,
And then, received each horse the needed care,
  Quick, o'er the plains, they scattered near and far.

They come!—and thundering down the red land slope,
  The fierce ganado‡ madly tears along,
While, close behind, urged to their utmost lope.
  The wild caballos§ drive the surging throng.
At headlong speed the riders keep the band,
  With yells and oaths, and waving hats and coats,
Till in the strong corral they panting stand,
  When, rest is gained for horses, and for throats.

Then comes the breakfast; soon the steer they kill,
  And quickly is the dressing hurried through;
The meat is cooked by rude, yet well-liked skill,
  And—all do know what hungry men can do.
The Patron sits beneath yon old oak tree,
  Encircled by a group of chatting friends:
For, at Rodeo all one can eat is free,
  And all around in greasy union blends.

* Jaquima (Hackemore) is the name given to a species of halter much used by Mexicans. It usually serves in place of bit and bridle, in breaking wild horses.
† Lariat, Reata, or Lasso, is the name of the rope used in picketing out and catching stock, and for a hundred other purposes. It is commonly made of horse hair, or raw hide; varies in length, and is a quarter of an inch thick. It has a running noose at one end, and is regarded by stock men and vaqueros to be as much a necessary part of the proper equipment of a rider and horse as the saddle itself.
‡ Ganado,—a band of horses or cattle.   § Cavalya,—horses.

The breakfast finished, cigarit's alight.
    Unto the huge corral all hands proceed ;
The strong-wove sinches are made doubly tight,
    And the renta's noose prepared for need.
The fire is kindled, and the iron brand,
    Amid its coals, receives the wonted heat;
The Patron waves assent, with eager hand,
    And the dark riders bound to saddle seat.

Where yon dark cloud of dust is rising high.
    The swart vaqueros, like the lightning, dart ;
And singling out their prey with practiced eye,
    Rush him from the affrighted herd apart.
Then whirls the lasso, whistling through the air,
    In rapid circles o'er each horseman's head,
Till round the yearling's throat is hurled the snare,
    Burning like a huge coil of molten lead.

Then, heedless of its struggles to get free,
    They drag it to the Major Domo's* stand,
Who, though of tender heart he's wont to be,
    Now, merciless, sears deep in its flesh the brand.
The Spanish mother, at her youngling's cry,
    Comes charging down with maddened hoof and horn—
While far and wide the crowd of gazers fly,
    And hide behind the fence-posts till she's gone.

In faith, it is a sight well worth to see,
    For those who love excitement's feverish touch ;
And he who can look on and passive be,
    Has ice within his nature over much.
What frantic bellowings pierce the startled air,
    What clouds of dust obscure the mid-day sky,
What frenzied looks the maddened cattle wear,
    As round and round, in vain, they raging fly.

These things, and many more, tend well to fill
    The eager cravings of a morbid mind :

* The overseer or boss.

Akin to passions that full oft instill
    Feelings that prompt the torture of its kind ;
But he, who rashly seeks a closer view
    Of tortured calf, to mark each groan and sigh,
Receives, full oft, rebuke in black and blue,
    Pointed, with force, to where his brains most lie.

The last calf now has met the common fate ;
    Ear clipped, and branded, they have set him free,
The crowd have left, a few alone do wait,
    And we have seen all that there is to see.
Perhaps, some day, by some far abler pen,
    These things shall, o'er again, be better told,
And strangers to our clime shall mark them then,
    And deem them far from either tame or cold.

THE "SHAKER."

Since the day when Eve first opened a style,
By donning a fig-leaf garb, the while ;
Each year some peculiar *mode* has had,
That set the women all running mad
    To be of its charms a partaker.
But all the years that have seen a "run,"
Are thrown into the shade by '61 ;
And completely is darkened the noted shine
Of Bloomer, Red Petticoat, Crinoline,
    By the bonnet *a la* "Shaker."

Bonnets of silk, and fine bonnets of straw,
Flats, hats and hoods, of patterns a score,
Have each been the *rage*, and passed away,
To give to some other gear the sway,
    With more of oddity on it.
But of all the articles ever displayed
On the heads of matron, or of maid ;
The ugliest, meanest thing of the pile—
Of a horrible shape, and an antique style—
    Is the confounded "Shaker" bonnet.

Better the sun should darken the neck,
Better that tan the cheek should fleck ;
Better the looks of each freckle and speck,
Than this thing with which the ladies deck
    The cranium's upper story.
It is shaped like a coal-scoop upside down,
With sooty ribbons trimming it round ;
And feebly dyed to a yellowish hue,
With a joint behind, and a scollop, or two ;
    And lo ! the feminine glory !

If the sect, from whom it takes its name,
Should by chance cast eyes upon the same
Kinds. that on our streets appear.
I'll bet two to one, without a fear,
    They'd have a grand " kerniption."
For in all the years that have passed away
Since the time of Eve, it's not rash to say,
That the eye of mortal never saw,
In all of the world. a thing before,
    Just answering its description.

Now take my advice, dear ladies, pray.
And throw the odious "Shaker" away ;
Contrive some bonnet—I'm sure you can !
That'll help your looks, and so please man.
    Which should be your firm intention.
None of those things that smother the hair
And render ugly what God made fair ;
But a nice little bonnet, janty and neat,
With ribbons, wax-flowers, all complete—
    Some charming bit of invention.

GRAINS OF GOLD.

Grains of gold! grains of gold!
Out in the day-dawn gray and cold,
Delving beneath the frost-bound mold,
For the scattered grains of glittering gold.

Through the sleety day, through the freezing night,
'Neath the blazing sun, in the pale moonlight;
'Mid the summer's bloom, and the winter's blight,
I have worn away life for these grains so bright.

An aching head and a mangled limb,
And an eye that a blast has rendered dim;
A shrunken arm, maimed, wasted and slim,
With a fever, that makes my brain to swim;

Rheumatism gnawing at every bone,
Consumption wheezing in every tone,
Are all that remain to me alone,
The grain I have reaped from the harvest sown.

Oh God! how I toiled for those grains of gold!
Conscience was seared, and honor was sold,
And heaven was lost, in the battle bold
I waged against fate, for her crumbs of gold.

Gold is the God of my native land!
Gold the best gift of the bridal hand;
And gold is the link of the brotherly band
That welds into friendship, or weakens to sand!

In the sunny years of my boyhood's life,
In days of peace, and in nights of strife,
Radiant with bliss, or with sorrows rife,
My eyes have turned to one star of my life:

Hair of gold ! hair of gold !
Beautiful, lifeless, shining and cold ;
My darling sleeps 'neath the church-yard mold,
The fairest flower its hillocks enfold !

A saddened memory of hours flown,
Of a love-lit eye, and a voice whose tone
Was the sweetest music my ear hath known,
Thrills me, and kills me—I'm poor, and alone!

An earnest and prayerful hope of rest ;
A simple picture chained to my breast,
Of her who was ever my angel best,
Are all that are mine in the golden West.

A BIRTH-DAY REVERIE.

I am out in the deep, cold gloom, to-night,
   With the years that have passed away and flown,
Musing in secret o'er the rapid flight
   Of hours I once had counted as my own ;
And Memory's bloodless hand, so thin and cold,
   Snake-like about my heart is tightly twined,
Awhilst its fingers steadily unfold
   The past, with malice but too well defined.

The cold drops gleam upon my icy brow,
   As, up from out the dark depths of the past,
Those things of yore, in a continuous flow,
   Sweep through my brain like a keen winter blast,
Oh, for one tear ! my eyes are parched and dry ;
   Long years have dragged their snail-like course away,
Since in their depths did soothing tear-drop lie,
   Or down my cheek, in moisture fade away.

Fond friends were once enshrined within my heart,
   But they've been torn from it, one after one ;
It was my fate, though hard, that we should part ;
   And now, of them, to me remaineth none.
I have not led a life—nor never may—
   Such as can either win, or keep a friend—
Shut up within myself, I've lived alway
   A prisoner to my nature—ne'er to blend.

When life's fair morn glowed on my boyish brow,
   And I was full of youth's bright, tinsel dreams,
Beauty became my god, and, even now,
   I bend the knee when on my sight it beams.

c

'Tis destiny! Thus, superstition's slave
    Worships the image graven out of stone,
And deems him blest, if its rude feet to lave,
    His brains around the idol's seat are strewn.

And this has been my curse! My mind has teemed
    So oft with phantom shapes of what it sought,
Has seen so much unlike those things it dreamed,
    That now it hath no faith or hope in aught.
The beauty that it worshipped, never yet
    Has been what it would have it, nor e'er will;
The real ne'er equals what the thoughts beget—
    The painter's brush outdoes e'en nature's skill.

Nature is man's sole law—and it is mine;
    But still, its teachings vary in each one;
I act as Fate do bid me—few divine
    Its end; but, as it ever bids me shun
The ways, that most have taken as a rule,
    As all are served who differ from their kind,
They call me crazy, or, worse yet, a fool;
    Unto their own queer conduct wholly blind.

The Turks have styled this Destiny, and say,
    That on man's brow it is all written clear;
On mine 'tis furrowed, and I dread, each day,
    To see another page of that dark lore appear.
The one, beneath whose fiat I now bend,
    Is pitiless in power and dread in might—
God, alone, knows how that long page will end,
    Or whether healed will be this deadly blight.

He, who doth wage a war against his fate,
    Is mad! far more than he who owns its sway;
Strife never can its iron grasp abate,
    Or, drive one single woe it dooms, away.
Far better then, to quietly submit
    To its decrees, howe'er they rack the breast,
In hope that Death ere long will conquer it,
    And bless its victim with an endless rest.

A score, and four, of years have passed away,
    And left me what? A broken, shattered thing;
A ball with which rude circumstances play,
    And here and there, as suits their caprice, fling.
But yet, I wait, and *sometimes* hope—for what?
    Let Heaven answer; it, alone, can tell
Whether the boon I crave shall be, or not,
    Or, unborn years bear still the stamp of hell.

MAGGIE, MAVOURNEEN.

Maggie, Mavourneen, the night stars are paling,
   Their beauty grows dim at the dawning of day ;
The Spirit of Gloom, through the cold air long sailing,
   To the lone mountain glens has hastened away.
Awake, Awake ! With thy brown hair loose flowing,
   From thy lattice gaze forth on the rosy young morn,
Which on thy fair cheek a light kiss bestowing,
   Will leave a new beauty to grace it, ere gone.

Maggie, Mavourneen, the wild lark is bringing
   A tribute of song to the merry red morn ;
The bright pearly dew-drops, to the wild flowers clinging,
   Have dropt from their bosoms, and faded, and gone.
Awake, oh, awake ! From thy soft sleep upspringing,
   Unlace the long lashes of thy dreamy eye,
Which o'er thy soul a rich glory flinging,
   Will reflect back the smiles that beam from the sky.

Maggie, Mavourneen, while all nature is teeming
   With beauties, no mists arise now to mar;
On thy angel-watched couch thou'rt silently dreaming—
   The sweetest of morn's lovely beauties, by far.
Awake, awake ! Soon the sun will be sweeping,
   O'er yon mountains of snow, in a torrent of wrath ;
One kiss from his lips will banish thy sleeping—
   Maggie, Mavourneen, linger not in his path.

SCENE IN THE TROPICS.

Slow the shades of eve are stealing
    Through the balmy, dreamy air ;
Silvery vesper bells are pealing
    Forth the call to evening prayer ;
And the light-winged zephyr, sighing
    O'er the sleeping, star-lit sea,
Wafts, from where the day is dying,
    Low, soft strains of melody.

Fragrant orange groves are sending
    Forth a perfume, rich and rare ;
Thither, joyously, are wending
    Dancers, dark-eyed, bright and fair ;
And the guitar's silver tinkling
    Softly swells the trees among,
Setting roguish eyes a twinkling,
    As their songs of love are sung.

But the shadow's growing dimmer,
    Where the moon-beams strike yon tree;
And a strange light's feeble glimmer
    Breaketh o'er the moaning sea.
Hark ! the distant thunder booming!—
    Every moment drawing nigher;
See the ink-black storm-clouds looming,
    Deeply tinged with lurid fire.

Along the wave-lashed, quaking shore
    The shivered trees are falling fast :
And, high above the tempest's roar,
    Shrill shrieks of pain, thrill on the blast,
From ruined village, grove, and fane,
    Where, through the long dark hours of night,
The storm-fiend of the hurricane
    Sweeps onward with resistless might.

Slow dawns, at last, the morning light,
    Revealing scenes of wildest dread ;
And all that bloomed so fair o'er night,
    In ruins, now, is blighted spread.
And, where the guitar's witching breath
    Floated, at eve, the trees among,
Stretched out in cold and mangled death.
    Full many a beauteous form is flung.

The church, where hung the vesper bell,
    Whose silvery tones so charmed the ear,
Heard, 'mid the blast, its hoarse death knell,
    And lies, a pile of ruins, near.
Peru's dark daughters long will mourn
    Above their lovely sisters' graves ;
With many a cross, they'll, shuddering, turn
    To where the blighted Orange waves.

PLOW DEEP.

Down in the depths of the musty old tome,
    Did the eyes of the student pore ;
Seeking amid the volume's rich loam
    The kernels of precious lore.
And large was the harvest knowledge sent,
    The student's mind to o'er heap,
As a glad reward for the time he spent
    In plowing her pages deep.

Fathoms beneath old ocean's blue wave,
    The intrepid diver sank;
And, standing within that mighty grave,
    Drew wealth from Death's "Saving's Bank."
Coin, and jewels, and gold he bore
    Back, on his upward leap;
For great the richness of ocean's store,
    To be found by plowing deep.

When moistened the earth by genial rains,
    The farmer prepares his land ;
From early dawn till twilight wanes,
    The plow seldom leaves his hand.
Deep tilled the soil—the buried grains
    To life, in the rich loam, leap ;
Soon a heavy crop rewards the pains
    Of the farmer in plowing deep.

'Twill thus be seen that he who would gain
    Fame, wealth, or a heavy crop,
Wherever he seeks them, seeks in vain,
    If he goes not beneath the top.
Light plowing is but poor work, at the best,
    Then, point the plowshare in steep ;
For, he with fortune is always blest,
    Who seeks it by plowing deep.

MARGARET LEE.

I'm kneeling within the church-yard to-night,
Where they've laid thee, my pretty Madge Lee;
My arms are thrown round thy tombstone white,
I droop o'er the mound that hides thee from sight—
    Oh! beautiful Margaret Lee!

Oh! this life is a weary one of mine,
Since thou hast left me, my darling Madge Lee;
For the smile that has fled from thy lips I pine,
For the joy of the voice, that so sweet, was thine—
    Oh! dark-eyed Margaret Lee!

Once, I was happy, *too* happy, when thou
Looked thy fond love, my worshiped Madge Lee;
But a hand of ice on my wrecked heart, now,
Is pressing its fingers, and chilling my brow—
    Oh! wildly loved Margaret Lee!

Oh! why didst thou leave me thus sadly alone,
To seek thee in heaven, my own Madge Lee?
Didst thou not know, when *thy* spirit had flown,
Drooping to death would then be my own?—
    Oh! brown-haired Margaret Lee!

The night winds come moaning around thy tomb,
Cold, cold as thy brow, my lost Madge Lee;
And the damp mists are blending in with the gloom,
But I heed not their poisonous breath of doom—
    I'm coming! sweet Margaret Lee!

O, joy! the blood in my veins grows cold!
On thy grave my head sinks slowly, Madge Lee;
From thy tombstone white my arms unfold.
I'm falling asleep on the church-yard mold!—
    Going!—going!—to—Margaret Lee!

A MYSTERY.

Strange are night's visions, that around the brow
Fold their wild wings, and nestle in the breast ;
Of mystic fabric are our dreams composed,
And deep within the heart they find a rest.
Perchance, these things are in the book impress'd
That holds our destinies, of which the mind,
Set free, by sleep, from the dull, cloddish breast,
Soaring far upward, leaves the earth behind,
And reads a portion — to all the balance blind.

Ah, who can tell their purpose or explain
Their mystic meaning? 'Tis beyond man's skill ;
Noiseless they come, and noiseless go again ;
And one creates a charm, the next doth kill ;
Filling the soul with hope or fear at will.
I, too, have dreamed, of late, a strange, wild dream ;
And pondered o'er its shape and form until
My brain has throbbed, nor caught a single gleam
To light the darkness that enwraps that dream.

As on my couch, in slumber stretched along,
I careless lay, one moonlight summer night,
A form of brightness, garbed in robes of gold,
Anear my pillow closed its pinions white.
And with a pen of flame it seemed to write,
Upon a silver tablet, words of gold,
That glowed like fire upon my dazzled sight ;
Then in a sweet, low voice it did unfold
Its state and purpose, as you here behold.

" From yon bright orb, where Venus sits enthroned
On radiant piles of silver and of gold,
And guides the timid eve and forward morn,
As they the gates of night and day unfold,
Lighting the stars with twilight flame of gold,

Quenching their lustre with the morning dew,
Hither I come, unto this lower world,
To do those things that I was bid to do,
Whose sibyl mystery, Fate may explain to you.

" As from you star my white wings cut their way,
I paused to look upon this restless sphere,
Which mortals call their own—in foolish pride—
And saw a form of beauty sleeping here,
Which, deeming strayed from heaven, I floated near.
Amid the milk-white linen of her bed
She nestled, and so lovely did appear,
That even I hung 'raptured o'er her head,
And half forgot the work for which to earth I sped.

" Upon the pillow streamed her dark-brown hair—
A shadow soft upon a mound of snow—
Falling from off a brow that clear and fair,
Rivalled the neck which sheened the hair athro'.
One arm, on which the blue veins traced the flow
Of the rich blood, beneath the ivory skin,
Was resting 'neath a cheek, with health aglow,
Shrouding the eyes long lashes latticed in,
And drooping o'er her neck the fingers long and thin.

" I linger'd for a moment, ere I sped,
Gazing upon the beauties there displayed,
Then culled a tress from off her lovely head,
And brought it hither, as my Queen hath bade,
For beauty thus hath licensed beauty's raid."
The spirit finished, and I saw it hold
The silken tress, once worn by that fair maid,
Unto my hand, which shortly did infold
The beauteous strands, finer than threads of gold.

Unfolding its long wings of snowy light,
The spirit vanished, softly as it came ;
And, then, again lit up the startled night,
A brilliant column of supernal flame,
To which the light I'd seen before was tame.

From out a cloud of mingled fleece and haze,
A melody, like chime of church bells, came;
And while the room seemed all around ablaze,
Voices of spirits thus this chant did raise :

CHANT.

"Thou art holding a lock of silken hair—
Have a care! have a care! beware!
Clipped from the head of maiden rare,
But blonde or brunette, dark or fair,
Whisper it, lock of hair!

"Be she old or young, short or tall—
Have a care! have a care! beware!
Dwells she in cottage, or in hall,
Loveth she much, or none at all,
Whisper it, lock of hair!

"The serpent hides in the lily's breast—
Have a care! have a care! beware!
He glistens when the wind is at rest,
But will he not sting when his coils are press'd?
Whisper it, lock of hair!

"A ring of gold, and a serpent, too—
Have a care! have a care! beware!
This little tress shall pass into,
But which of the twain is meant for you;
The future will declare."

  * * * * *

I twined the silken, dark-brown tress of hair
Around my finger in a single fold ;
It glowed, as though afire, a moment there,
Then changed into a little ring of gold—
But soon again its former shape did hold.
I placed it in my bosom, and it wore
A serpent's form, and slimy grew, and cold ;
It raised its head to strike ; its tongue I saw,
And woke—my dream, and night were o'er.

The day had dawned, when from my sleep I broke,
And mid-way up the morning-gilded sky,
Venus had veiled her glories in a cloud,
And every star had sought its couch on high,
While the red sun the horizon was nigh.
My dream I thought of as fled with the night;
But springing from my couch, there caught my eye
A little coil, which glistened in the light—
A lock of hair!—a mystery of the night!

FOR MUSIC.

When sorrow o'er thy young heart is stealing,
   And grief on thy brow casts a shade,
As blighted by this world's cold feeling,
   The flowers of thy bright dreams fade ;
Oh, turn to the cage where is biding
   The sweet bird your heart holds so dear ;
Perchance, in his gay song there's hiding
   Some charm that will banish each tear.

When in anguish thy head is low bending,
   As life's star shines darkly and dim;
And tears from thy pure heart are wending,
   Till in pearl-drops thy bright eyes swim ;
Oh, turn to the cage whence is welling
   The music so sweet to thine ear ;
Perchance, in the melody's dwelling
   Some charm that will banish each tear.

When loved friends are coldly forsaking
   The heart that they never could prize ;
And in silence thy young spirit's breaking,
   And thy breast runneth over with sighs ;
Then turn to the pet bird that's flinging
   Around thee a melody dear ;
Perchance, to some note there is clinging
   A charm that will banish each tear.

The soul that in sorrow is pining,
   Oft a solace in music can find ;
As round it each fond note is twining,
   Every grief at once flies from the mind ;
When melody around it is stealing,
   As soft as the light, summer air ;
There will come to thy soul a calm feeling,
   That drives from the eye every tear.

LITTLE "BELLE BEAUTY."

Dark-eyed child with the midnight hair,
    Thy merry laugh's sweet silv'ry peals,
Into this weary heart of mine,
    Like a half-forgotten music, steals ;
And, as with thy little frisky pet,
    You while the hour in graceful play,
The accents of thy soft voice ring
    With the vanished charm of another day.

I have sat and watched thy nimble foot
    Go tripping it lightly to and fro ;
I have marked the sunny smile-beams flit
    From thy rosy lips to thy brow of snow ;
I have seen thy dark hair's glist'ning curls
    Float out, like down, on the Autumn air ;
Then fall, like feathers of jet on snow,
    Back to thy neck of a whiteness rare ;

And I've thought of one as fair as thou,
    Who nestled anear me, in boyhood's day,
But whose bright dark eye and lute-toned voice
    To the angel land are passed away.
Her merry voice hath oft made glad
    A brother's heart, with its girlish glee ;
Her face was so like to thine, bright child,
    No wonder I love to gaze on thee !

May *thy* life, so glad in its early morn,
    Through years, and years of happiness run ;
May the same bright smile, that I saw to-day,
    As merrily greet each morning's sun !
May the tomb ne'er steal, as it did from one
    Who faded away, oh, long ago,
The rose-tint from *thy* fair young cheek,
    Or twine thy brow with its wreath of snow !

Strangers are we; though the hand of Fate
    Has brought us, the while, each other anear,
We part, perchance, never again to meet,
    Nor more may thy sweet voice greet my ear;
Yet, its winsome tones will linger long
    In my heart, when thou art far away;
And thy sunny smile in my mind will gleam
    As bright as it wreathed thy lips, to-day.

ON THE ROAD.

Away! away! o'er the dusty plain,
With blood-stained spur, and a slackened rein,
With a muttered joy at each quickened bound,
I hurl my steed o'er the trembling ground.

The sun is sinking afar in the West,
The night-wind sweeps down from the mountain crest
The grey owl's wild eyes peer out from the grass,
And the bat wheels into the air as I pass.

Away! away! on his straining breast
The great cords swell and the foam is prest;
But the fire glows in the grey steed's eye,
And his breath comes hissing, hot, and dry.

On my anxious brow the sweat beads stand,
And fall like fire-drops on my hand;
But I shout like mad at the whirlwind speed,
To which I have urged my panting steed.

Away! away! I am into the night;
And the stars are out in their mantles white;
My blue steel spur is with red gore drent,
And half of the whip from my wrist is rent.

A stumble—a fall—and my horse is down!
But, with a wild snort, he springs from the ground;
I breathe him a moment—in saddle again—
And madly, once more, we tear o'er the plain.

On! on! the shadows in the road lie dark,
And echoes anear the cayote's bark;
But nor whip nor spur can know of a rest,
'Till the form I love is strained to my breast.

A SONG OF AUTUMN.

The leaves are sighing, sadly sighing
    The requiem of the dying year—
And dark-browed cloudlets slowly flying
    O'er the earth, drop down a tear.
Nature now wears a sombre face,
    As conscious that its smiles must fade,
When Winter rules, in Summer's place,
    From its cold throne enwreathed with shade.

The leaves are mourning, ever mourning;
    In silence all night long they weep;
Their gay green robes are slowly turning
    To the dark-brown garb of sleep.
The flowers that by the fountain dwelt,
    When smiled the merry Summer sun,
The change that's coming, too, have felt,
    And droop their crumbling stems upon.

The leaves are falling, thickly falling;
    On the ground they mouldering lie,
Or, upon the winds of Autumn,
    Round in freakish circles fly.
The little birds that once sang gaily,
    Peeping the green foliage through,
Now chirping hop amid them daily,
    Bidding them a long adieu.

My soul is musing, sadly musing,
    Within my little chamber here,
O'er the dreams that, too, are loosing
    All their brightness with the year.
The hopes that in my heart once dwelt,
    When smiled the morn of youth's bright sky,
The changeful hand of time have felt,
    And, like the flowers, but bloomed, to die.

L

My heart is wishing, often wishing,
    When sighs the wind so mournful deep,
That with earth's flowerets now fading,
    It, too, could droop and go to sleep.
For it is like the earth in winter,
    Its flowers gone, its song birds flown,
And barren as a frozen meadow,
    Where Gloom hath reared his ebon throne.

SECRET GRIEF.

The smile around the lips may play,
    The eye may flash with merry light,
And still the heart be far from gay,
    Nor teem the mind with visions bright ;
A joyous look the face may wear,
    And lightsome words the tongue may speak,
The brow may show no trace of care,
    Nor shade of sorrow blanch the cheek ;

Yet, still, within the silent breast,
    A fire of anguished thought may burn,
Whose searing flame ne'er knoweth rest,
    Or smoulders in its living urn ;
A weight of grief that none may know,
    Is hidden in each smother'd sigh ;
From eyes and lips wells forth a woe,
    That finds no vent when man is nigh.

The mirthful song, the flash of wit,
    To other ears may seem as bright,
As though some one had uttered it,
    Whose heart had never known a blight.
The eye that oft in moisture swims,
    Reflects a sorrow, light and brief ;
But not a tear the vision dims,
    To tell the pangs of secret grief.

But, when alone, the breaking heart
    Unburdens from the breast each care,
And thrilling sighs unbidden part,
    The thin, cold, silent wreaths of air ;
When from the icy brow there spring
    Tears, that with anguish gleam and glow,
And fleeting minutes seem to bring
    Upon their wings an age of woe ;

When every thought breathes but despair,
    When every scene is tinged with gloom,
When the soul's ceaseless, only prayer,
    Asks but the rest found in the tomb ;
When hope's sweet promises are shed,
    Upon an ear to solace deaf,
The heart to joy, life, all, is dead—
    All, but its own consuming grief.

MORE LIGHT.

More Light! more light! is the student's sigh,
    As low o'er his book he doth pore ;
And wildly flashes his gleaming eye,
    As he gathers the priceless lore.
His lamp burns dim as the night breeze sighs
    Through the creaking and broken blind ;
But with iron will his task he plies,
    Gathering more light for the mind.

More light! more light! is the Christian's prayer,
    As he bows o'er the page of grace,
To glean the truths that are hidden there,
    And its wonders of love to trace.
In the closet hours of silent night,
    As he bends o'er the sacred scroll,
His prayer to Heaven oft wings its flight,
    In search of more light for the soul.

More light ! more light ! is the poet's cry,
    As he raises his aching head,
And wistfully gleams his bright, dark eye,
    As his spirit by dreams is fed.
His soul grows sick as the dark hours fly,
    And his brow is throbbing with pain ;
From his breast there breaketh a feeble sigh,
    As he seeks more light for the brain.

More light ! more light ! is the plaintive wail
    That sadly breaks o'er Afric's sea,
From lands where millions in darkness quail,
    Blind in their own idolatry.
With imploring voice the heathen turns
    To lands that Gospel light doth cheer ;
Dim in the distance the spark he discerns,
    And o'er the sea his shouts ring clear.

More light! more light! 'tis our greatest need,
    For life is short, the future dark ;
With doubt our souls must always bleed,
    'Till death shall quench the guiding spark.
And oft ascends the murmuring cry,
    From those who wander, wrapt in gloom,
Asking from Heaven the reason why
    Mankind must *blindly* meet their doom.

TEARS.

How beautiful a blue eye looks,
  Seen through a vail of tears !
How brightly, when the grief is past,
  The sweet smile reappears !

Thus, oft, the night-sky's softest blue
  Through some fleece-vail will sheen ;
And moon-beams, as the cloud drifts by,
  Smile sweetly o'er the scene.

Tears are the dew-drops of the heart :
  From its deep cells they spring ;
When care and grief a blight impart,
  They fall and soothe the sting.

Tears are the fairest, richest gems
  Sweet maidenhood can wear ;
No jewels grace earth's diadems,
  More lustrous, pure, and rare.

Tears are the mind's own rays of light :
  When darkly throbs the brain,
They flash, and through the mental night
  It brightens up again.

They nestle on the young girl's cheek,
  Like dew on flowers, the while
In beauty, till the eyes look down,
  And melt them with a smile.

Tears are the soul's warm, summer rain :
  When hope has nearly fled,
Its fading bloom returns again,
  As those warm drops are shed.

EUNINE.

Far off in the distant East.
    There's a glimmer of misty light,
As star after star quietly slips
    From out the numb grasp of Night.

We have watched them fade away—
    The shadows and I, from the plain ;
Thy star-bright eyes, like them, Eunine,
    Seemed brightest when on the wane.

When Day furled his banner of light,
    And left his world-charge to Sleep,
I wandered out 'mid the tents of Night,
    My watch for the lost to keep.

I made me a seat of brown moss,
    'Neath a tangled wild-wood vine,
And I gazed in the eyes of heaven, Eunine,
    As oft I have gazed in thine.

As I saw each star go down
    'Mid that ocean of moon-lit blue,
I thought of hopes that, once as bright,
    Had vanished as quickly, too.

Some madcap Spirit of light ;
    As merry and wild as thee ;
Out from behind the curtains of night
    Leapt down in smiles on me.

But quickly their brilliant light
    Faded away from my brow ;
So like to that of *thy* smiles Eunine—
    A bright memory only, now.

TO ADELLA.

Beautiful thought of a mind divine,
    Bright-eyed child of the voice of song ;
What echoes woke in this heart of mine,
    As o'er thy strain it lingered 'long.
Music was made for the saddened heart—
    A voice like thine, to soothe the soul ;
'Tis God's own gift !—in vain would art
    Seek thus man's spirit to control !

My mind was dark with things of the past,
    The stings of many a heavy blow ;
With dreams of friendship, ne'er to last,
    And much of ill that earth doth know ;
From thy lips there came a sweet, low strain,
    That charmed the ear with its gentle spell ;
It glowed in the heart, and soothed the brain,
    And calmed the breast's wild, angry swell.

I lingered long o'er that witching air,
    Till it died away in echoes sweet ;
And oft my mind, when dull with care,
    Bids memory the charm repeat ;
But in thy voice the spell is bound,
    And soothes not now, as once, the strain ;
My heart leaps up at music sound,
    And calls on thee to soothe—in vain !

Then, since thy voice man's woes can calm,
    Thy soul and it keep ever pure !
And let its gentle accents gush
    From out a heart no guile can lure.

Y

Thy brow is fair, for thy young mind
    On it, as yet, no pang has wrote;
And may the years to come ne'er find
    A sully on thy brow or note!

Sing on! but *never* tune thy voice
    To aught of ill; but let its charm ·
Soothe ever grief, and woe, and wrong,
    And ne'er be raised to scorn or harm.
So shall each one, as I do now,
    Whene'er thy gentle song they hear,
A blessing breathe upon thy brow,
    For moments thou hast rendered dear.

OF A VERITY.

'Tis strange that a sensible man should go mad,
　　When woman proves naught but a flirt;
There's more of the kind in the world to be had,
　　And as cheap, too, as dust and dirt.

The fish just drawn from the rivulet's breast,
　　By the fisherman's skillful hand,
Is not so much better than all the rest,
　　Left nestling still in the sand.

The first peach that falls from the laden tree,
　　That we eat with such pleasure now,
Is no sweeter than those that above, we see,
　　Bend low the stout old bough.

" The lovely Miss ——— is enriched with *such* charms ;
　　Her waist is a span in size ,
Perfection modeled her hands and arms,
　　And the Heavens colored her eyes ;"

But ten to one, were the truth but known,
　　The form, by " beauty so graced,"
Unpadded, would prove all skin and bone,
　　And her waist but tightly laced.

Another charmer is, oh ! *so* sweet,
　　With her words and honied smiles ;
But she gives them alike to all she doth meet ;
　　To catch fools, she expends her wiles.

Then take my advice and do not feel hurt,
　　Should your love but meet with scorn ;
For woman soon learns to be but a flirt ;—
　　With hearts they are rarely born.

IN DARKNESS.

Out in the silent night.
  Alone with a sleepless grief:
And I hear the sound of a much loved name
  In the rustle of every leaf.

The leaves dance on the tree,
  Or whirl to the river's brink :
They must be happy, for, not like me
  Are they cursed with the power to think.

I call to the dark-browed waves—
  What reward doth friendship meet ?
" Ingratitude, thou fool !" comes hoarsely back,
  As on their course they fleet.

'Twere well to be as a stone—
  A witless, senseless thing ;
To pass through the world to feeling unknown,
  Then memory could not sting.

The past is wrapt in a pall,
  And the future shrouded in gloom ;
And the face of heaven is black with a wrath,
  That hurls a relentless doom.

I turn to the stately trees—
  Can ye my anguish hear ?
A withered leaf falls down to my feet ;
  Ingratitude *thus* can sear.

Out in the silent night,
  Alone with a broken dream ;
And I see the smile of a shadowy face,
  In every pale moonbeam.

A LOVE SONG.

(TO MUSIC.)

Fondly the pale stars watch, love,
    Watch o'er the flowers asleep ;
And the silver wave with its snowy crest,
    Is catching the tears they weep.
Softly the dew-drops fall, love,
    Fall on the mossy green ;
And the leaves of the lily gently fold,
    With the sparkling drops between.

There's music in the air, love,
    Music for the heart alone ;
And dreams of love, too wildly bright,
    Breathe softly in each tone.
Sweetly the strains are played, love,
    Played by a fairy hand ;
And the soul grows sadder whilst it lists
    To the song of the sylphid band.

Sighing, I sit and dream, love,
    Dream 'neath the green-leafed tree ;
And my heart beats high in gladsome hope,
    That thou'rt dreaming, too, of me.
Sweetly the pale stars smile, love,
    Smile, in their quiet mirth ;
They know that deep is the love I bear,
    Their fairy sister on earth.

THE OLD MAID'S BURIAL.

'Twas dark midnight, along the way,
In heavy clouds the damp mist lay;
When in her noisome grave was laid,
A sour, wrinkled, crabbed old maid;
And those who stood by the coffin's side,
Chuckled to think of death's new bride.

An owl, perched on a tombstone white,
Hooted in scorn at such a sight;
And the slimy snake, that near did hide,
Hissed his contempt of woman's pride;
While those who bent o'er the old maid's tomb,
Saw devils and imps dance through the gloom.

"Go search," they said, "in the serpent's bed,
And bring the dead leaves to wreathe her head;
The poisonous night-shade we will lay,
To rot, on this mass of useless clay—
O! the worms below, that laugh at the sight,
Will feast to their fill, on old bones this night!

"Go catch the toad, 'neath yonder yew,
And take from its back the blistering dew;
Then, as the grave with sods you stop,
On each tuft of grass let fall a drop,
So that nothing green will wave above
The grave of one whom *none* could love.

BELLA DOWE.

(TO MUSIC.)

The pale moon-beams, with mellow light,
　　In dreamy silence crept
O'er a low couch where, calm and bright,
　　A child of beauty slept.
Many a tear of woe was shed
　　O'er her pale, marble brow,
From hearts whose cherished hopes had fled
　　With my lost Bella Dowe.

CHORUS.—Then scatter flowers o'er her grave,
　　　　The head in sorrow bow ;
　　　The little mound with tear drops lave,
　　　　Where sleeps sweet Bella Dowe.

Where flowers bloom the summer long,
　　Down by the brooklet's wave,
The oak tree bends its branches strong,
　　To guard my Bella's grave.
The violet and wild rose-tree,
　　When twilight shades their brow,
Droop their fair heads, to mourn with me
　　The loss of Bella Dowe.

When evening shades steal on apace,
　　And o'er the brown leaves creep,
I often roam to that sweet place,
　　Where Bella lies asleep ;
And kneeling by the little stone
　　That marks the spot, e'en now,
I muse on all the joys I've known
　　With my lost Bella Dowe.

MINNIE MAY.

(AIR—NETTY MOORE.)

In a little brown cottage,
When the busy day was o'er,
I have passed many happy hours away,
In gazing on the beauty,
And in list'ning to the voice
Of pretty, little, winsome Minnie May.

CHORUS—Then I miss you, Minnie May,
And my heart is sad to-day,
For the music of thy voice no more I hear :
All my happiness has fled,
And to joy my heart is dead,
Since no longer, gentle Minnie, thou art near.

Through the long and lonely hours
I have toiled with content,
For I knew that night was slowly drawing nigh ;
And when my work was done,
With a joy that naught could quell,
To that little cottage I would quickly hie.

In the silent hours of darkness,
As I slumber, all alone,
Oft I dream of thee, so beautiful and gay,
While angels seem to whisper,
Ever softly in my ear,
The cherished name of darling Minnie May.

From thy lips the smiles are gone,
And I look for them in vain,
While my heart is growing sadder, day by day ;
Shall I hear thy voice no more ?
Are the happy days all o'er?
Have I lost thee, then, forever, Minnie May ?

LOST.

With its dark wings flapping about my heart,
    A spectre, whithersoe'er I go,
    Is thrilling my brain with a cry of woe,
That pierceth my soul through, like a dart ;
    And as around me those wings are tossed,
    Wildly it crieth, *" Lost ! Lost ! Lost !"*

It comes when the shadows earthward hie ;
    And my pale soul turneth in affright,
    To hide from the cold, gray eyes of night ;
But, frightfully plain, 'tis ever nigh ;
    And round me, still, as its wings are tossed,
    Wildly it crieth, *" Lost ! Lost ! Lost !"*

It haunteth the sunshine smiles of day ;
    And my soul is learning to curse the light
    That brings no relief to the woes of night.
With my heart-strings its sharp talons play ;
    And around me as its wings are tossed,
    Wildly it crieth, *" Lost ! Lost ! Lost !"*

Must that spectre grim, with its terrible might,
    Till the end of life thus torture my heart,
    Withering, and blighting with demonish art ?
Can no charm be found that this fiend will affright,
    And still those wings that around me are tossed,
    And hush that wild cry, *" Lost ! Lost ! Lost ?"*

Yes, there's a charm !—but in vain I seek—
    A spirit of light—of power divine,
    That can soothe this all-killing woe of mine,
That can turn to a heaven this world so bleak ;
    But, between me and it those wings are tossed ;
    And thrilleth that cry of—*" Lost ! Lost ! Lost !"*

6

LOST.

Oh, Spirit of beauty, love and light!
 Pity me! save me! stretch forth thy hand!
 For the spectre will fly if *thou* wilt command.
Leave me not longer to struggle in night;
 But over my heart let *thy* pinions be crossed,
 And whisper, " *Found! Found!* oh, nevermore *lost!*"

THE DAUGHTER'S SACRIFICE.

(FROM THE LADY OF LYONS.)

Father! my heart is breaking now,
    The bloom has left my cheek;
The damps of death are on my brow—
    Hush, father!—do not speak!
Thy limbs in prison ne'er shall rest;
    Thy child will grateful prove;
I'll still the woe within my breast—
    But, *talk no more of love!*

Father! my thoughts are turning now
    To yon white-tented field;
To him who gained the only vow
    My *heart* can ever yield.
'Tis hard to tear it thus from one
    It holds all else above—
Father—no more! thy tears have won—
    But, *talk no more of love!*

Father! the thing thou bidst me wed
    I hate! oh, how I hate!
Revenge and spite—not love—has led
    Him thus to choose a mate!
Be still, my heart! thy pulse I'll chain!—
    Down! down! thy strength I'll prove!—
Father! 'tis done! but, ne'er again,
    Talk to *me* of *his* love!

Father! I'm calm—I'm *very* still!
    My tears, thou need'st not fear!
My heart *must* bear this grievous ill—
    'Twill save thee, father, dear!
One moment—let me kneel in prayer
    To the kind Heaven above—
I'm r-e-a-d-y—n-o-w—the bond prepare—
    But, *talk no more of love!*

NO MORE.

My soul, thy dreaming cease, awake!
   'Tis folly to longer hope;
Thy air-built castles of joy will break,
   And leave the with grief to cope.
Dreams are naught but spirits of night,
   That joy's bright garb oft wear—
Their smile is sweet, but leaves a blight
   In the heart, when they disappear.

My heart, thy sighing cease, forbear!
   'Tis folly to longer pine;
There's none for thy sorrows e'er will care,
   No sympathy e'er be thine.
There's few can read thee aright;
   Those few smile at thy despair;
But though they may treat thee with despite,
   My heart from thy sighing forbear.

My brain thy throbbing cease, and rest;
   'Tis folly to longer work;
The pictures by fancy on thee impres'd,
   Are teeming with naught but murk.
Fancy's pencil touch is but light,
   Soon pales its colors gay;
The sketch will fade when brought to the light,
   Then away with thy dreams, away!